Printed in Wales by
Stephens & George Print Group,
Goat Mill Road,
Dowlais,
Merthyr Tydfil,
Mid Glamorgan,
CF48 3TD.

Tel: 01685 388888
Web: www.stephensandgeorge.co.uk
Email: sales@stephensandgeorge.co.uk

Cover: W/free Silk Coated 250gsm
Text pages: Woodforce Silk 130gsm

The HAIRY PLUG MONSTER

Published by

HPM MEDIA LTD
25 Windermere Drive
Alderley Edge
SK9 7UP

Reg. 06807611

ISBN 978-0-9563320-0-4
First Published Author House 2009
Second Edition HPM MEDIA Ltd 2009

This book belongs to:

....

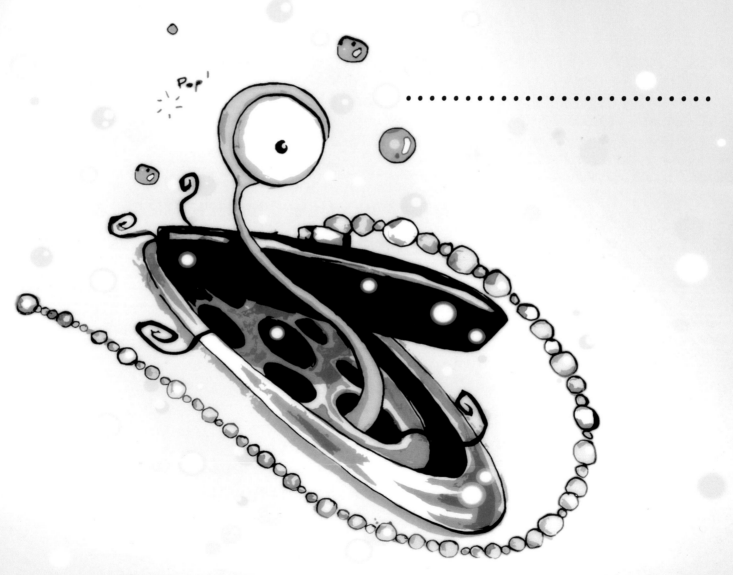

Produced by Kul Cuthbert for HPM Media Ltd
With special thanks to Laura and Fiona

Email: info@hairyplugmonster.com
Web: www.hairyplugmonster.com

For Arisha-Jane, Maya-Rose and Yulia
With love xxx

"What's that noise
in the bathroom?"
Maya said with a shout.
"There's a noise from the hole
where water runs out!"

"Don't worry about that!"
said her Dad with a laugh.
"That's The hairy plug monster!
who lives under the bath."

"The hairy plug monster
what's that?" Maya asked
as she moved her head closer
and peaked in the bath.

"He drinks the bath water
with a gurgling sound,
he has one big wide eye
that spins round and around."

"A bubble bath sandwich
each night for his snack,
with a dollop of soap
that he rubs on his back."

"A bubble bath sandwich!"
she said with a roar,
then bent down to listen
for a sound from the floor.

The hairy plug monster,
was there underneath
with a mouthful of shampoo
for cleaning his teeth.

With a gurgle, a guzzle,
a gulp and a slurp,
he drank the bath water
then did a huge burp

"It's now time for bed"
said her Dad with a grin,
then kissed her good night
and tucked Maya in...

All comfy and snug,
Maya lay there in bed
and thought of the monster
and the things that Dad said.

A bubble bath sandwich
it can't taste that nice
not even with chips,
or spaghetti or rice.

"I know what I'll *do*"
she thought to herself,
"I'll make him a snack
with the food on the shelf."

And slowly she tiptoed
across the floor,
past Dolly and Teddy
away through the door.

She crept into
the bathroom,
and pulled up
the plug
and quiety
whispered

"Glug,
   glug,
      glug,
         glug,
            glug"

"BURP!" Went the bath
and from out of the tap
The hairy plug monster
squeezed
through the gap.

He looked up at Maya
and said "How do you do!
I'm The hairy plug monster,
pray tell... who are you?"

"Hello back again"
said Maya with charm,
as she held out a towel
at the end of her arm.

"I've come to invite you
for dinner downstairs,
we can eat lots of biscuits
and chocolate éclairs."

Maya asked with a grin
"Do you fancy a feed?"
The hairy plug monster
Smiled and agreed.

They slid down the banister,
crept through the hall,
then into the kitchen
to the shelf on the wall.

The shelf it was
laden with biscuits
and sweets,

Maya stood on
her tiptoes
but still
couldn't reach.

Maya thought and then said
"I know just what to do
if you stand on the table
then I'll stand on you!"

Maya stood on his shoulders
and reached for the tin,
lifted the lid
and slid her hand in.

With a smile she passed down
a handful of chocs,
then the chocolate éclairs
that were still in the box.

With a gurgle, a guzzle,
a gulp and a slurp,
he ate all the choclates
then did a huge burp.

After the feast
it was time for a nap,
so he crept back upstairs
and squeezed back
through the tap.

"What's that noise?" said her Dad,
the next day, with a shout.
"There's a noise from the hole
where the water runs out!"

"Don't worry about that!"
Maya said with a laugh,
"that's The hairy plug monster
who lives under the bath!"

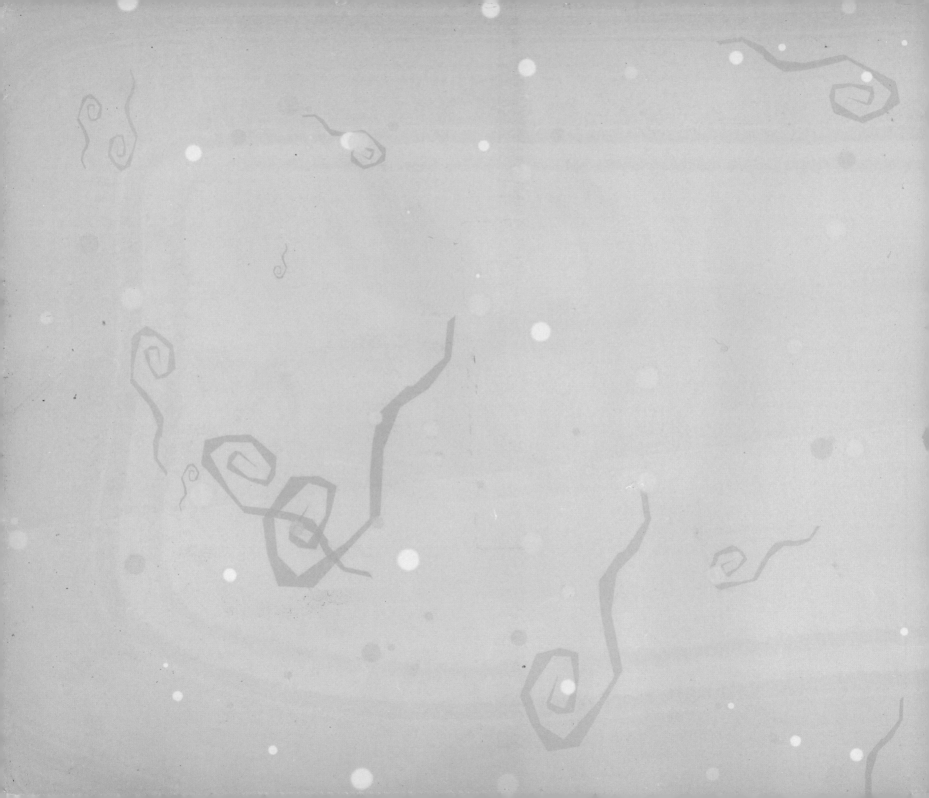